LIGHTHOUSE

A Story of Remembrance

For Sarah Gillis, Antigonish, Nova Scotia.
— R.M.

For my husband, Chris, with love always, and with thanks for his support.
Thanks also to my models, Juliana and Pat.
— J.W.

The illustrations for this book were painted in oils on canvas.

This book was designed in QuarkXPress, with type set in 15 point Goudy Old Style.

Text copyright © 2003 by Bob Munsch Enterprises Ltd.
Illustrations copyright © 2003 by Janet Wilson
Title page drawing copyright © 2003 by Sarah Gillis
All rights reserved. Published by Scholastic Inc.

SCHOLASTIC, CARTWHEEL BOOKS, and associated logos are trademarks and/or
registered trademarks of Scholastic Inc.

Library of Congress Cataloging-in-Publication Data

Munsch, Robert N., 1945-
   Lighthouse : a story of remembrance/ by Robert Munsch ;
illustrated by Janet Wilson.
      p. cm.
Summary: After her grandfather's funeral, Sarah wakes her father in
the middle of the night so they can go to the lighthouse her grandfather
loved and remember other nighttime visits there.

   ISBN 0-439-49031-6 -- ISBN 0-439-49032-4 (pbk.)
   [1. Memory--Fiction. 2. Fathers and daughters--Fiction. 3.
Grandfathers--Fiction. 4. Lighthouses--Fiction.] I. Wilson, Janet,
1962- ill. II. Title.
   PZ7.M927 Li 2003
   [E]--dc21
                                                2002013714

Parent Shelf - Death
JE

10 9 8 7 6 5 4   03 04 05 06 07
                           Printed in Canada
                    First printing, September 2003

Robert Munsch

LIGHTHOUSE

A *Story of Remembrance*

Illustrated by

Janet Wilson

Cartwheel
·B·O·O·K·S·®

SCHOLASTIC INC.
New York Toronto London Auckland Sydney
Mexico City New Delhi Hong Kong Buenos Aires

*I*n the middle of the night, Sarah woke up, put a
flower in her hair, and went into her mother and
father's bedroom. She sat on her father's side of the
bed for a long time. Finally he woke up and said,
"Sarah, what's going on? It's the middle of the night."

"Well," said Sarah, "you always told me how
Grandpa used to take you out to the lighthouse in
the middle of the night, and this is the middle
of the night, and tonight is the night to take me."

Her father lay still for a long time, and then he said, "Yes, I think this is the night."

So they got dressed very quietly, went out to the car, and drove off.

There was nobody else around.
No cars were out, and the
streetlights made the sea
fog glow.

"When Grandpa took me to
the lighthouse there were no
streetlights, and there were no
doughnut shops open in the
middle of the night," said
Sarah's father.

"But he would have stopped
if there had been doughnut
shops," said Sarah.

"Right," said her father.

So they stopped at a doughnut shop and bought a bag of maple icing doughnuts and some coffee. They were the only customers there.

"When I was little, Grandpa used to give me coffee, and it always tasted terrible," said Sarah's dad.

So they both drank some coffee for Grandpa. Dad's coffee tasted good, and Sarah's coffee tasted terrible.

Then they drove out of town
till they came to the road that
led to the lighthouse.

"Grandpa always said we
should walk up the road to
the lighthouse," said Sarah's
father.

"Right," said Sarah.

So they parked the car and
walked up through the fog to
the lighthouse.

Then they sat on the top of
the cliff above the beach and
listened to the waves crash
on the rocks. Sarah ate the
doughnuts, and her father
drank more coffee.

"All the times Grandpa took me with him," said
Sarah's father, "we never once went up to the top of
the lighthouse. The door was always locked. We tried
to open it, but it was always locked."

"I'm going to try the door," said Sarah.

So she walked over and tried the knob, and the
door opened. Sarah and her dad stood looking at
the doorway.

"What now?" said Sarah.

"Grandpa would have gone up," said Sarah's father.

"So let's go up," said Sarah.

They walked up the winding staircase,

round and round and round and round,

until finally they stood in front of the light.

"I can see forever," said Sarah. "Can Grandpa see me?"

"I don't know," said her father.

"Can Grandpa hear me?" said Sarah. And she yelled really loud, "GRANDPA!"

They waited a long time.

"He's not going to answer," said her father.

They stood for a long time
and listened to the foghorn
and looked at the mist and
the ocean. Then Sarah took
the flower from her hair, the
flower she had saved from
her grandfather's funeral,
and threw it way out over
the ocean.

"When I grow up, I'm going to have a kid, and someday we will come here in the very middle of the night," said Sarah.

"Right," said her father.

And then, covered with dew from the fog
and smelling like seaweed, they went
home to bed.